BIG APPLE BARN™

HAPPY'S HOLIDAY

by **KRISTIN EARHART**

Illustrations by
JOHN STEVEN GURNEY

SCHOLASTIC INC.
New York   Toronto   London   Auckland   Sydney
Mexico City   New Delhi   Hong Kong   Buenos Aires

To the Robinetts — Marilyn, Stan, Hali, Ty, and Spencer —
the perfect family with whom to spend the holidays,
even when I didn't get the biggest piece.

— K.J.E.

ISBN-13: 978-0-545-01774-9
ISBN-10: 0-545-01774-2

12 11 10 9 8 7 6 5 4 3 2 1   7 8 9 10 11 12/0
40

Printed in the U.S.A.
First printing, November 2007

Contents

WELCOME TO
BIG APPLE BARN!

Chapter One

Winter Is on Its Way

"Hold still, Happy," Ivy Marshall said to the quarter pony.

Happy Go Lucky's skin twitched. He turned to look at his favorite rider. How could Ivy expect him to hold still? He was itchy all over!

"It won't be long now," Diane Marshall said to Happy. Ivy's mom was the riding trainer at Big Apple Barn. With the help of her daughters, Ivy and Andrea, she took care of all of the ponies and horses at the barn. Now she was stretching a measuring tape across Happy's back. As the tape brushed against Happy's long winter coat, it ruffled his hair. Happy stamped. He swished his tail. When Diane and Ivy walked away for a moment, he sighed.

"Be patient, Happy," Goldilocks advised. The caramel-colored pony was watching from her stall. "You just need to relax."

"That's easy for you to say," Happy replied. "I have all this hair and it tickles! I need a good brushing."

"Yes," Goldi said, tossing her blond mane out of her dark eyes. "But Diane needs to measure you for your new winter blanket. If you move, you'll mess things up. You don't want a blanket that doesn't fit, do you?"

Happy rolled his eyes, but he knew his friend was right. She was older than Happy, and she understood the way things worked around the barn. That didn't make it any easier to stand still, though. All he really wanted was to scratch his back!

It was the first cold week of the winter, and Happy's hair was already thick and long. It always took him a while to get used to having more hair. In the summer, his coat of hair was sleek and smooth. It was so soft, Ivy would pet him for hours. But his winter coat made him feel scruffy. No matter how much Ivy or his other riders brushed Happy, they could never get all of the dirt away from his skin — and that made him itch!

"Of course, you won't get as itchy if you wear a blanket," Goldi said as if reading

Happy's mind. "It will keep you cleaner, for starters. And it will stop your hair from getting thicker."

"I don't think his coat could get any thicker," an appaloosa pony nearby added with a flip of her mane. The pony's name was Sassafras Surprise, though everyone called her Sassy. She was always willing to offer her opinion. "Happy already has more hair than any pony I have ever seen. He's like a giant guinea pig!"

"Very funny, Sassy," Happy groaned. "Just because your stall is next to Goldi's doesn't mean you can butt into all of her conversations." Then Happy snorted in a huffy way, but he wasn't serious. He liked Sassy, and she was right. He kind of felt like a giant guinea pig — a giant guinea pig that needed a blanket.

Happy didn't know why he had to grow such a thick winter coat. At his old barn, he hadn't minded as much. There, he could go outside all winter long, so his hair kept him warm. But at Big Apple Barn, the ponies stayed inside when it became really cold. Happy wasn't looking forward to being cooped up until spring. He liked the fresh air and loved to see snow. Just thinking about having to stay inside all winter made him nervous. He stamped his hoof and twitched again.

5

"You're doing great, Happy," Ivy said, returning to Happy's side and running her hand along his neck. Ivy always knew how to make Happy feel better. She leaned close to his head and tickled behind his ear. Happy could smell something sweet on her breath.

"That's it," Diane announced, rolling up the measuring tape. "If all goes well, you'll have your blanket before Big Apple Barn's holiday party."

Ivy smiled. "Just wait here," she whispered to Happy. "I'll get you a treat."

After Ivy was gone, Happy looked at Goldi. "We're having a holiday party?"

"Oh!" Goldi exclaimed. "You two haven't been here for the Christmas Eve open house

6

before. It's one of the best things about being a school pony at Big Apple Barn."

"Really?" Sassy asked. "I love parties! Who's invited?"

"All of the ponies and horses, and all of the riding students and their families," Goldi said. The three ponies were part of Diane's riding school. Diane taught kids how to ride and the ponies helped. "Everyone comes to wish us happy holidays. The children bring apples and carrots. Diane serves candy canes and hot apple cider, and," Goldi added with a sly smile, "the students sometimes sneak a nibble or two our way."

Happy's eyes grew wide. He had never had a candy cane. Once, on his birthday, his old owner had given him a cube of sugar. Happy still remembered how the little square of sweetness had melted on his tongue. He had never tasted anything like it!

"Are there games?" Sassy asked. "Every party should have games."

"Not really," Goldi said. "It's just fun to see the children so happy, and to see the barn decorations. Plus, they play music. Holiday music!"

"Now you're talking," Sassy declared. "I'll be there with bells on."

Chapter Two

A New Rider for Happy

Happy looked out over his stall door. He was waiting for his new rider. Happy loved to get new riders! First of all, they were almost always sweet and excited. Even though they might not know how to ride a pony or brush a pony or even walk next to a pony, they always wanted to learn.

And, sometimes, new riders were shy. Happy understood why. He could be shy when meeting new horses and people, too. Happy had been a new lesson pony not that long ago. Now he was really good at working with all different riders. Ivy was still his favorite, but he was glad to know so many of the kids who came to Big Apple Barn.

As Happy watched the door at the other end of the barn, a tabby cat padded up to his stall. A young mouse with shiny white teeth scampered behind her.

"Hello, Happy," the cat said.

"Hey, Happy," the mouse chimed in. "It's getting chilly, isn't it?"

Happy nodded at his friends in turn. "Hello, Prudence," he said to the cat. "Good to see you, Roscoe," he said with a smile to the mouse.

"You're getting a new rider today, Happy?" Prudence asked with a flick of her tail.

"Yes, a little girl," Happy said. "I hope she likes me."

"Oh, your riders always love you," Roscoe assured him. "And they give you the yummiest treats." Roscoe raised his eyebrows at the pony and gave him a grin. Happy often shared his apples, grain, and other good food with the mouse. That's what friends were for.

"If I were you, I would hope your new rider doesn't like you *too* much," Prudence advised. The orange tabby's whiskers drooped and she gave Happy a long stare.

Happy cocked his head to one side. "What do you mean, Prudence?"

"I'm just saying that you have to be careful." The cat continued to look Happy in the eye. "People do rash things this time of year."

Happy was just about to ask what "rash" meant when the big barn door rolled open. The three friends watched as a girl, bundled up in a thick green coat, jeans, and rubber boots, slipped around the corner. Even from the other end of the barn, Happy could see the girl's jaw drop as she looked at all of the horses and ponies in their stalls. Her face was bright, and she glanced back over her shoulder. Her father appeared behind her.

"Oh, my. Would you look at that?" Prudence took a deep breath. "Happy, don't say I didn't warn you. This pair is trouble for sure," the tabby declared. Then she walked away, her nose high in the air.

"Roscoe," Happy began, "what does she mean?"

"I don't know," Roscoe said. "But that guy doesn't really look like he should be in a stable, does he?"

Happy had to agree. The man was wearing a long, tan coat with black pants. His shoes were shiny and his just-combed hair was sleek. Happy thought he looked like he would get dirty just walking down the aisle. Most people wore old clothes and old shoes when they came to the barn. It wasn't a fancy place! Happy nibbled on his lower lip. He didn't know why, but Prudence's words of caution suddenly made him nervous.

"Oh, Daddy," the girl said in a small voice, "they're all so beautiful!"

"They are, aren't they?" the man replied, taking his daughter's hand as they walked down the barn aisle.

"Oh, and look! A kitty!" The girl pulled away from her dad and rushed toward Prudence, reaching out her arms. Prudence stopped. Her tail became stiff. As the girl came closer, Prudence backed up, turned around, and leaped onto Goldi's stall door.

The girl stopped. "I'm sorry, kitty. It's okay," she said in a softer voice. But

Prudence did not look back. She dug her claws into the wooden door frame and dashed up to one of the barn's roof beams. She paused to look down at Happy, Roscoe, and the new rider. Then she stalked away, high above them all, without a single meow.

Happy was relieved when Diane appeared. "Don't mind Prudence. She takes a while to warm up," Diane explained. She reached out, and the girl put her small pink glove in Diane's hand. "Welcome to Big Apple Barn. You must be Nell," the trainer greeted her. "I'm Diane."

"Hi, Diane," Nell said. "I like your barn."

Diane laughed. "I'm glad. I hope you'll like Happy, too. He's the pony you will ride."

"I'll like him," Nell said quickly. "I just know I will."

As Diane led Nell toward Happy's stall, the pony looked over at Roscoe.

"See, she's going to like you," Roscoe said. "You don't have anything to worry about."

Happy tried to smile.

Roscoe leaped from the door to the feed bucket and then to the ground. "Don't forget to save me a bite of your treat," he called before he scurried away.

Happy wouldn't forget. He wouldn't forget Prudence's warning, either.

Once the lesson had started, Happy was able to enjoy himself. It was Nell's first time on a pony. To start, Diane walked next to Happy while he carried Nell around the ring.

Next, Diane attached a long line to Happy's bridle, and Happy walked around Diane in a circle. It was a safe way for Nell to get used to being in the saddle and holding the reins.

Happy tried to keep a smooth pace, so that the ride was easy and fun for Nell.

The whole time, Nell's dad watched from the side of the ring. His smile was as bright as his shoes, which Happy noticed had not yet gotten dirty. Happy looked over at the man several times. He wanted to figure out why Prudence thought that Nell and her dad were trouble, but he didn't have a clue.

Later, after the lesson, Nell's dad came up

to Happy's stall. "Well, sweetheart," he said, turning to Nell, "what do you think of the pony you rode today?"

"Oh, he's just lovely," Nell said. "Don't you think so?" She patted Happy on the nose.

"I certainly do," her dad replied. "So you'd be *happy* to ride him again?" Happy noticed how the man had said *happy* loudly. It had sounded bigger than the other words.

Nell smiled. "Daddy, are you trying to be funny?"

Her dad laughed lightly. "Maybe just a little."

"Yeah, I would love to ride him again. I really like Happy," Nell said. She pulled a couple of carrots out of her bag. "Do you think he likes me?"

At the sight of the carrots, Happy nickered.

"He likes you. You got it right from the horse's mouth," Nell's dad said.

Nell rolled her eyes. "That one was a stretch," she said. "My dad likes silly jokes," she whispered to Happy so her dad could still hear. Her father shrugged his shoulders and smiled.

"Come on, honey," he said. "Give Happy his treats so we can head home."

Happy tossed his head up and down. He didn't care what Prudence said, he liked this guy! And Nell, too. The carrots she'd brought were long, and they still had the greens attached. He would have plenty to share with Roscoe. When Nell held up a carrot, Happy whinnied. "Do you like me or the carrots?" Nell questioned, grinning.

Happy pushed his nose playfully against Nell's shoulder.

"Well, okay then," Nell said as she fed Happy. "You can have the carrots anyway."

Chapter Three

One Last Field Day

The next day, Diane put Happy out in the field with his friends. Since it had gotten colder, Happy had not seen as much of the other horses and ponies. He sometimes saw Goldi and Sassy in the barn aisle or during lessons. But he rarely had the chance to see Big Ben. He missed him especially.

Big Ben was Diane's show jumper, and his

stall was at the other end of the barn. Happy only saw the older horse when they spent time together in the pasture. Big Ben was more of an advisor than a friend. He was wise, and Happy knew he didn't say things just to be nice. Happy could always count on Big Ben to tell him the truth.

That afternoon, Goldi and Sassy were talking about the Christmas Eve open house again. Sassy wanted to hear about all the presents Goldi had received from her lesson riders in past years. While Goldi answered questions, Happy was able to talk alone with Big Ben.

"Well, now," Big Ben said, "how are you, Happy?"

"I'm good," Happy replied. "It's great to see you."

"Are you enjoying your lessons?" Big Ben asked.

"Oh, yes. I got a new rider yesterday," Happy shared. "She was really nice. Prudence didn't think I would like her, but I did."

Big Ben looked thoughtful. "She didn't, did she? Why was that?"

"Oh, I don't know," Happy said as he sniffed the ground in search of some green grass. "She said something about people being 'rash' this time of year." Happy lifted his head, realizing that Big Ben might be able to explain. "Do you know what that means?"

"Well, yes," Big Ben began. "'Rash' can mean different things. But I believe Prudence was saying that people sometimes do things quickly around the holidays, without really thinking."

"Oh," Happy said. "Well, Nell was very thoughtful. She even brought me carrots with tops." He bent back down to try to find something to eat, but the ground was cold and the grass tasted dry.

"Good, then. I trust Nell isn't rash," Big Ben said. Then he took a deep breath. "The air is so crisp and refreshing today. If it only stayed like this, we could probably come outside all winter long. But soon it will be too cold."

Happy paused. "So it's true? We don't get to come outside until it's warm again?"

"It's true," the older horse confirmed. "Diane thinks it keeps us healthier if we stay inside where it is warm. She also doesn't want to worry about us sliding on ice or getting stuck in deep mud. As horses and ponies, we depend on Diane to know what is best for us. I think she does a good job."

"But we won't get to see snow," Happy said, his voice quiet. "Every year I wish on the first snowflake I see." He sighed and then looked up at Big Ben. "I loved watching the snow at my old barn. I didn't even have to go outside. I could see it from my stall. I'd watch it fall for hours."

"I understand. It's tough to spend the winter inside. At least at Big Apple Barn you have friends to keep you company."

"But how will we see each other if we're stuck in our stalls?" Happy asked, confused.

"Well, Diane lets us run in the inside paddock sometimes. We can't graze, of course. But it is good to stretch our legs."

Happy was relieved to hear that. He was lucky to have made so many friends at his new home, and it was good to know he'd still be able to see them during the winter.

All too soon, Ivy and her sister, Andrea, appeared at the field gate. "Time to come in!" they called. It was late in the afternoon and the sun was setting. Happy watched the other horses, including Big Ben, head toward the gate.

"Aren't you coming?" Sassy asked, turning to look back at Happy.

"I'll be right there. I want to be outside just one minute more," he explained. Happy searched the darkening sky. It felt cold enough for snow, but there was none in sight.

After all of the other horses were inside, Ivy returned for Happy. "Come on, boy!" she called. "I have a surprise for you."

Happy looked back toward the barn. He might not have snow this winter, but he would still have his friends — and his favorite rider, Ivy. And, for now, he also had a surprise!

Chapter Four

Not-So-Good News

"We've been busy," Ivy told Happy when he met her at the gate. "Mom, Dad, Andrea, and I all pitched in. I think it's the best year yet."

Happy was excited, but he had no idea what Ivy was talking about. Ivy smoothed her hand along his shoulder as they walked. As much as Happy loved the brisk air, he was looking forward to getting back to his warm stall. Now that the sun had gone down, it felt much colder outside.

"Are you ready?" Ivy asked as they neared the barn. Happy pricked his ears forward. As Ivy rolled the door open with a firm tug, a warm glow came from inside. Colorful lights were wrapped around the barn rafters, and wreaths made of hay hung on each stall. Walking down the aisle, Happy saw a hand-painted sign over the tack room door. It read, HAPPY HOLIDAYS FROM BIG APPLE BARN. And there were smaller signs on the stall doors that read, PEACE, JOY, HOPE.

"Happy, I'm so glad you're here," Ivy said as they walked down the barn aisle. "I can't wait for winter vacation. I don't have to go to school, so I can come to the barn every day and visit." That was good news to Happy. He loved being with Ivy. Even when she wasn't riding him, they still had fun. "Last year," Ivy went on, "I didn't have a special pony to ride, so winter vacation was kind of boring. But now that you're at Big Apple Barn, everything is better."

Happy nuzzled his nose against Ivy's hair and she giggled. "Well, here we are. Do you like it?" she asked.

Happy turned to his stall and saw that there was a hay wreath hanging above his door, and a patchwork stocking on the door itself. Across the top of the stocking, his name was stitched in green.

"I made it myself," Ivy said. "It's full of alfalfa cubes for you and candy canes for me." Ivy smiled as she pulled out a cube and fed it to Happy. Then she opened up the stall and let Happy walk inside. After she latched the door, she reached for the stocking again. This time she selected a piece of red-and-white-striped candy. As she unwrapped it, Happy took a big sniff. He had noticed that sweetness on Ivy's breath before.

It smelled delicious! Happy pricked his ears forward.

"You want some more alfalfa?" Ivy asked, handing him a square. Happy lipped it from her fingers. It might not be candy, but alfalfa was still tasty. "I have to get ready for dinner now," Ivy said. "Good night, Happy!"

Ivy walked to the end of the aisle and turned off the lights. Happy could hear the barn door scrape against the ground as Ivy left. Then he heard something else. It was a rustling, and it sounded like it was coming from his stocking!

"Don't worry, Happy," a small voice called. "It's just me, Roscoe! I hid in here before Ivy stuffed it with alfalfa and candy canes. I'll be out in a sec."

Roscoe eventually climbed to the top of Happy's door. "Oh, Happy," the tiny mouse panted. "I feel like I've been waiting all day. You'll never believe what I heard."

Happy looked down at his big-eared buddy. Roscoe was always overhearing things and telling the rest of the barn.

"I bet I'll believe it," Happy said. "But you can still tell me."

"It's not like that," Roscoe insisted, hands on his furry hips. "This is serious."

Happy looked into his friend's dark eyes.

They did not sparkle the way
they usually did when he
had big news.

"What is it?"
Happy asked.

"Well, I can't
say for sure." Roscoe
paused and took a breath. He whispered,
"But I think someone wants to buy you."

Happy put his ears back. "But I'm not
for sale," he insisted. "Where did you
hear that?"

"That man. Your new rider's dad. You
know," Roscoe said, gesturing. "The tall
one with the long coat. And the funny
jokes."

Happy had not thought much of the
man's jokes, but he knew who Roscoe
meant. Nell's dad.

"What makes you think he wants to buy me?" Happy questioned, still uncertain.

Roscoe frowned. "I heard him talking to Diane. He said he wants to get something very special for Nell for Christmas."

"Well, that doesn't mean he wants to buy *me*," Happy insisted.

"I know, I know. But you are the pony that Nell is riding. And you know how he jokes around and likes to play with words. He said he wanted to find something that would make Nell very *happy*," Roscoe said. "And your name *is* Happy." Roscoe looked at his friend and raised his eyebrows. "Plus, why else would he be talking to Diane, if the gift didn't have something to do with Big Apple Barn?"

Happy didn't answer Roscoe's question.

"Well, what do you think?" Roscoe tried again.

"I don't know what to think," Happy replied. He stared blankly into the dark aisle. "What did Diane say?"

"I don't know," the mouse admitted. "They started walking toward Diane's house and I couldn't hear their voices. Their footsteps were too loud."

"Well, I don't want to be sold, but what can I do?" Happy asked. "I'm not going to worry when we don't even know if he was talking about me."

"Oh, he was talking about you all right," someone chimed in.

Happy searched all around for the voice. "Prudence, what are you doing up there?" he asked.

The cat glowered down at him from an overhead beam. "Remember when I warned you?" she asked. "This was just what I was afraid of. People do things like this around the holidays. They buy big gifts without thinking," she explained, whipping her tail around in disgust. She began to pace. "People don't think about the fact that having a pony is a lot of work. A pony needs food, brushing, exercise, and love. People don't take the time to consider that. They just think what a cute present a pony makes, all pretty with a big red bow."

Happy blinked. He had never heard Prudence say that much at once, especially not with so much feeling. She always had opinions, but she hardly ever got upset.

"Do you think Diane will sell me? Even though Ivy rides me?" he asked.

"I wouldn't put it past her. You can never know what a person will do," Prudence declared.

"Maybe not. But what are *we* going to do?" Roscoe asked.

Chapter Five

Sassy's Two Cents

The next day was Happy's weekly lesson with Ivy. He usually enjoyed this day more than any other. He liked being with Ivy, and he liked learning more about working together. That's what lessons were all about, and Diane always gave them good advice. Lately, Happy and Ivy had been jumping more. With each lesson, Diane set the fences higher and Happy had more fun.

But today something felt different. It wasn't because Andrea and Sassy were sharing the lesson, either. Happy didn't mind that at all. It gave him a chance to catch up with his appaloosa friend.

But he wasn't interested in talking today. How could he chitchat when he kept thinking about what Roscoe and Prudence had said? The mouse and cat were sure that Diane was going to sell Happy to Nell's father. Now it was all Happy could think about.

While Diane was setting up the fences, Ivy and Andrea rode the ponies into the center of the ring and waited to begin their lesson.

"Hello there, Happy," Sassy greeted him.

"Hi," replied Happy, without looking in Sassy's direction.

"Well, it's nice to see you, too," Sassy

grunted. Then she put her ears back, to make sure Happy knew she was annoyed.

With this, Happy turned to the appaloosa. He knew he should tell her why he was in a bad mood, but he couldn't bring himself to talk about it. Instead, he lowered his head and sighed.

"Okay, Ivy," Diane called, "let's see what you and Happy can do."

Happy sighed again and tried to gather the energy to jump the course. He felt Ivy sit up in the saddle and gather the reins. Then, just as he stepped forward, he felt something else. *Ouch!*

A sharp pain shot through Happy's hind-quarters, and he bolted forward.

"Sassy!" Happy heard Andrea yell in a harsh tone.

"What happened?" Diane asked, stepping up next to Happy and Ivy. She glanced from one pony to the other.

"Sassy bit Happy," Andrea said in disbelief.

Happy stopped and looked back toward his tail. He thought he could see teeth marks in his furry coat! Then he stared at Sassy. She did not look the least bit sorry.

Ivy quickly climbed down and checked to see if Happy was okay. She fussed over him as she ran her hand along his hindquarters.

"Sassy, that's not like you at all," Diane said, walking toward the pony and shaking her head.

"I know," Andrea agreed. "She and Happy are usually great friends."

"Happy looks fine," Ivy reported. "She just gave him a nip." Ivy patted Happy again before she pulled herself back into the saddle. The bite didn't really hurt anymore, but it had shocked him. Now Happy knew he *had* to talk to Sassy, or else he'd have another thing to worry about.

"Ivy, you and Happy looked good today," Diane said at the end of the lesson.

"Thanks, Mom," Ivy said. "Happy always gives it his best." Ivy bent down from her spot in the saddle to pat Happy's neck, and Diane smiled at the pair. Happy couldn't believe Diane would sell him. He and Ivy were such a good team! It made him sad to even think about it. How could Diane do that to him or to Ivy?

Ivy tugged lightly on the reins to ask Happy to stop at the side of the ring and then dismounted. When she took off his saddle and saddle pad, steam rose as the sweat on Happy's back hit the cold air. Now that it was winter, Ivy put a special blanket on Happy when she cooled him off after a long ride. The blanket was called a cooler, and it kept Happy from catching a chill while he was still wet with sweat.

Just then, Sassy and Andrea walked up. Andrea chatted with Ivy as she removed Sassy's saddle and spread a cooler over the appaloosa's back as well. "You want to walk together? I'll make sure Sassy doesn't try anything funny," Andrea promised.

Ivy nodded. "We need to talk about Mom's and Dad's Christmas gifts," she said. The two sisters set off around the ring with the ponies following behind.

"What's up with you?" Sassy asked.

"Me?" Happy responded. "I'm not going around biting my friends!"

"It's true. I bit you," Sassy admitted. "Although I regret it."

40

"You do?" Happy asked.

"Well, yes," Sassy said matter-of-factly. "I'm sorry because I ended up with a gob of your hair in my mouth. It was revolting! You are one hairy pony."

"But *why* did you bite me?" Happy questioned.

"Because you ignored me," Sassy explained with a toss of her mane. "You seem upset, and I want to know why. You're my friend."

Happy knew she had a point. She was his friend, so he should tell her. "I *am* upset," he confessed. "Roscoe overheard a man talking about giving his daughter a Christmas present, and Roscoe thinks the present is me."

"Really?" Sassy asked. Her voice sounded excited.

"Really," Happy answered. His voice was

very serious. "I mean, it might not be me. But the girl is my new rider, so Roscoe and Prudence think Diane is going to sell me."

"Wow," Sassy said, her eyes sparkling. "Can you imagine being a Christmas present? They'll probably put a big velvet bow on you. If it were me, I would want a red one. I look good in red."

Happy nodded. Sassy did look good in red. But that wasn't the point!

"Then, when the little girl sees her perfect new pony," Sassy continued, almost in a daydream, "her face will light up in a huge grin — all because of you!"

Happy looked at his friend in disbelief. "But I won't get to be a school pony anymore. And I might have to leave Big Apple Barn," he argued.

"But you'll be a Christmas present. There's nothing more wonderful than that," Sassy insisted. "I would love to make someone that happy."

Happy shook his head. "Christmas is just one day. A new owner and a new barn last much longer than that. Remember when you were new here? It took a long time before this felt like your home."

"Well, you're right about that. And I know how much you like it here," Sassy agreed. "But, I have to say, if someone gave me a red velvet bow, I would feel at home pretty fast."

Chapter Six

The Gift of Christmas Past

The next day, Roscoe and Prudence paid Happy a visit in his stall. Roscoe slid under the door, and Prudence jumped over. Then Roscoe took one last look down the aisle to make sure no one was snooping.

"We know what to do," the mouse announced. "We know how to keep you from being sold."

"You do?" Happy asked, full of hope.

"Yep," Roscoe said. "It'll be a piece of

cake." The mouse snapped his fingers and looked over at Prudence. "Can I tell him?"

The tabby gave Roscoe the hint of a nod.

"Okay," Roscoe said, rubbing his hands together. "When's your next lesson with Nell?"

"Um," Happy thought out loud. "It's on Wednesday."

"That's just two days away! Perfect," Roscoe declared. "Now listen closely. It's very simple. All good plans are." Roscoe looked Happy in the eye. "When Nell comes in on Wednesday, be mean." He paused for a moment to let it sink in. "That's right. Be mean to her. Be mean to her dad. Be mean to everyone."

"Be *mean*?" Happy questioned.

"Yessirree." Roscoe nodded. "Whatever you do, don't be nice. If you're mean, they'll never want to buy you!" Roscoe looked over at Prudence, who gave him another slight nod.

"Well, that *is* a plan," Happy told his friends. "And I appreciate your coming up with it for me," he added with a shrug.

"But?" Roscoe prompted.

"But I can't do that," Happy explained. "I can't be mean to Nell and her dad on purpose. They've been good to me."

"Happy," Roscoe said with a scowl, "do I have to remind you that your life as a Big Apple Barn school pony depends on this?"

"Maybe so," Happy said, "but I just can't do it. I like being nice." He gave Roscoe a small smile, and he thought his friend understood. Then he looked at Prudence. She did not understand.

"There's nothing wrong with being nice, Happy," Prudence began, her whiskers drooping. "But there is also nothing wrong with looking out for yourself." She lifted her chin and twitched her nose. "I will tell you why." The tabby had a matter-of-fact tone. She looked straight ahead, and continued talking.

"It was holiday time, many years ago. I was a kitten, and a cute one at that. The very first man who came to the house picked me out of the whole litter. He said I was the perfect present for his son and daughter." She sighed, looking down at the ground. "I was perfect for about two days. Then I made a mistake. I didn't know how to use a litter box and no one was around to put me outside. It wasn't long before the parents agreed that I was too much work for the

47

family. And I was sad, because I really liked the children."

Happy and Roscoe exchanged glances. They had never heard Prudence talk about her past before. They just thought that she had always lived at Big Apple Barn.

"Diane found me out in front of her house. She took me to the vet and helped me gain weight. When I was healthy again, she brought me to the barn to meet the horses. I was just supposed to visit and then go back home with her, but I made it clear that I wanted to stay in the barn. I did not want to live in a house. I did not want to depend on a family for all of my food and comfort. Not if all that could be taken away."

Prudence's voice trailed off as she stared into the darkness. Then she blinked and lifted her head high. "Living in the barn, I learned very quickly how to take care of myself. And now that I am older and wiser, I look after my friends, too." She walked up to Happy and wove herself around his legs, rubbing her chin against his knee. "You're a nice pony, Happy," she said, her tone soft and honest. She was being so sweet and quiet! It was very out of character for Prudence and it made Happy a little nervous. Still, he lowered his head to hear her better.

Prudence walked right up to Happy's face. Then she raised a gentle paw to the pony's nose and said, "I don't want what happened to me to happen to you."

Without another word, Prudence leaped to the top of Happy's stall door. From there, she jumped onto the roof beam and slinked into the evening shadows. Happy and Roscoe were alone.

Happy didn't know what to say. It was such a sad story, but if that family had not given up Prudence, he never would have met her. He was glad to have her as a friend. And she seemed to belong at Big Apple Barn. He couldn't imagine her living anywhere else.

Happy felt he belonged at Big Apple Barn, too, with Prudence and Roscoe. Sassy, Goldi, and Big Ben. Diane and Ivy. Now he just had to figure out how to make sure he could stay.

Chapter Seven

Sassy's Second Stand

"I'm going to run away," Happy told Sassy the next day before their lesson. Their riders were already in their saddles, ready to go.

"What?" Sassy asked, turning to look at her friend. "Are you kidding? That will never work. What are you thinking?"

Happy was about to explain his plan to Sassy, but then Diane called to her students. "Okay, Andrew and Sasha," she said, "walk your ponies to the outside of the ring. Then ask them to trot."

Happy looked over his shoulder at Sassy. He wanted to tell her that he'd explain everything later, but her rider had already turned her in the other direction. He hoped they would have time to talk at the end of the lesson, so he could find out what Sassy thought of his plan. He had brainstormed for hours with Roscoe and Prudence. Now he needed another opinion.

As Happy trotted around the ring with Andrew on his back, he went over the plan in his head. First, Roscoe and Prudence would figure out how to unlock Happy's door. Next, on the night before the open house, they would spring Happy from his stall. Then Roscoe would take Happy to his nest in the hay barn. Roscoe promised Happy that he could hide there as long as he wanted.

That way, everyone would *think* Happy had run away.

Andrew was a new rider, so Happy was not concentrating very hard on the lesson. He was so caught up in his thoughts that he didn't notice Sassy trotting up behind him.

"Run away? Are you crazy?" she asked as her long stride brought her up to Happy's side. "You can't just leave!"

"Sasha," Diane called to Sassy's rider. "Why don't you turn Sassy and cut across the ring. Don't let her trot so close to Happy."

Sasha pulled on the rein to turn Sassy, but the appaloosa pony was stubborn.

"Happy, you have some explaining to do," Sassy insisted, keeping step with her friend. "You'd better not go back to your stall without talking to me." Sassy hurried to fit in all her words before Sasha yanked her head away.

Happy could tell that Sassy meant business. She was his friend and wanted to be able to tell him what was on her mind.

Happy was relieved when the lesson was over and Sasha led Sassy over to him and Andrew. The two students usually walked together while the ponies cooled down. Now Happy would be able to tell Sassy how the plan worked. He realized that she had misunderstood.

"Happy Go Lucky, you should know that running away won't solve anything," Sassy announced before Happy could say a word. "Remember when I tried to run away, and you came to get me out of the deep, dark woods? That place was spooky. It would be even scarier at this time of year, with no leaves on the trees and the cold wind always blowing." Sassy shivered just thinking about it. "Anyway, you know that it is always better to face your problems, not run from them."

Happy agreed with Sassy. He was going to say so, but she kept talking.

"Do you know that it's freezing cold out there? You don't even have your blanket yet. You might like snow and all, but being alone in the  cold with no place to go is *not* a good plan."

Happy wanted to tell Sassy that she was right, but she would not give him a chance!

"Happy, I don't want you to have to move to another barn. But if you run away, you still won't be at Big Apple Barn. I'd miss you. And think of Roscoe. Oh, and especially Ivy." Sassy shook her head. "You don't even know that you are being sold for sure."

Sassy was making a lot of good points. The most important one was that Happy did not know if he was actually being sold or not. No one knew what kind of present Nell's dad wanted to get for her. Roscoe had just heard that he wanted to find a present that would make Nell truly *happy*.

Happy was impressed with how much Sassy had thought about his plan! But just as he thought he would get a chance to tell Sassy the whole story, he heard Sasha click her tongue.

"Come on, Sassy," Sasha said, "let's go back to your stall."

"Wait!" Happy said, but Sassy was already heading back to the main barn.

"Don't do anything rash!" Sassy called before she was out of earshot.

That was the last thing Happy wanted to do.

Shortly after Andrew put Happy back in his stall, Roscoe stopped by for a chat.

"I'm so glad to see you," Happy told the mouse. "You have to talk to Sassy for me. You have to explain the plan. She thinks I'm going to run and hide in the woods."

"It's okay if she thinks that, isn't it?" Roscoe asked.

"No," Happy insisted, "I don't want her to worry."

"But if you tell everyone, it won't be a secret," Roscoe said, his hands firmly on his hips. "And then the plan won't work."

"Can you just tell her?" Happy begged. "Please?"

Just then, Ivy peeked her head over the door. "Hi, Happy! You wouldn't want an apple, would you?" she asked.

Happy glanced at Ivy and then gave Roscoe a final pleading look.

"Oh, all right," the mouse grunted before huffing away.

"Oh, there's your mouse friend," Ivy said. "Hello, little mouse." She paused, watching Roscoe scurry off before turning back to Happy.

"So, do you want this apple or not?" she asked.

Of course he wanted the apple! Happy nickered and stepped closer to the front of his stall. He stretched out his neck and took a deep breath. He could smell the sweetness of the apple. When he tucked his lips around it and took a bite, the tangy juice filled his mouth. What a treat!

"Happy," Ivy said with a giggle, "you act like it's candy!" As she spoke, her face lit up. "While you have your apple, I'll have a candy cane." She reached into the stocking on Happy's door and pulled out a red-and-white cane. "This is one of the best parts of Christmas," Ivy told him. "Candy canes and snow. If I can have those two things, it feels like Christmas to me."

Happy agreed about the snow. He could not believe a whole winter was going to go

by when he wouldn't see the world all covered in white. He would not get to wish on the first snowflake, either.

"And it wouldn't feel like Christmas without you here, either, Happy," Ivy added. She scratched the pony behind his ears.

Happy suddenly felt bad. Despite what Sassy had said, he still believed he had to run away. Yet he worried about how Ivy would react when she saw his empty stall. She might think that he had run away because he wanted to escape Big Apple Barn, but what he really wanted was to stay.

"Your new blanket should be here in time for the Christmas Eve open house," Ivy said. "You'll look so nice for the party. I can't wait to see you in your blanket."

Happy sighed. If everything went according to plan, he would not be at the Big Apple Barn party.

Chapter Eight

Nell's Secret

The next day was Nell's second lesson. Happy felt funny when he saw her walk into the barn. He had been talking with Roscoe and Prudence about Nell all week. Now that she was there, Happy remembered how sweet she had been the first time he met her. He realized it would not be bad being her pony. She would be a good owner.

She was already a good rider. Happy was surprised, since it was only her second lesson. Nell had soft hands, which meant that she could tell Happy where to go without tugging too hard on the reins. It showed that she wanted to work with Happy, not just tell him what to do.

When the lesson was over, Nell gave Happy a long brushing. Happy loved being groomed. Nell seemed to know all the best places to brush. Now Happy thought maybe he shouldn't run away. It might hurt Nell's feelings. *She would be nice to me,* Happy told himself. *But if I am Nell's pony, Ivy won't be allowed to ride me.* Happy did not want to have to choose!

Nell made little circles on his back with the curry brush. The brush helped pull loose hair from Happy's thick coat. Happy leaned toward Nell, so she would scratch exactly where his back was itchy. As she worked, Nell chatted. "This will make you all clean for the party tomorrow," she said.

Happy looked around to study Nell's face. She was smiling. "You know what?" Nell asked. "I have a secret. I know what one of my presents is."

Happy swallowed.

"I'm so excited," Nell continued. "I told my dad what I wanted. He said that it would take a lot of responsibility, but I know I can do it. He does, too." She bent over and searched through the brush box until she found a short metal comb. She stood up and ran the comb through Happy's black mane. "My dad said he trusts me to do a good job." Nell's voice was full of pride.

"Well, I'm done. Now you're nice and clean," Nell announced. She smiled again, then reached into her bag and pulled out a few carrots with the greens attached. "My

dad is probably waiting outside, so I have to go," she said after giving Happy his treat. "Bye — happy holidays!" Then she giggled. Her laugh sounded like short coughs. "It's funny saying happy holidays to you, because your name is Happy. My dad always makes jokes like that." She waved. "See you tomorrow!"

As she turned to walk away, Nell tripped over Prudence, who had been sitting outside

Happy's stall. The tabby cat squawked as she flipped over on her back, legs thrashing in the air. Before Prudence could get back on her feet, Nell dropped to her knees.

"Oh, Prudence! I'm so sorry," Nell said, her voice warm and soothing. Prudence rolled over and scowled at the girl. But the scowl quickly faded.

"You don't have to run away," Nell said. "I won't pet you if you don't want me to."

Happy could tell Prudence was confused. She would usually only let Ivy pet her.

"But I *could* pet you," Nell offered. "If you wanted. I could scratch behind your ears or rub under your chin." When Prudence didn't dart away, Nell slowly reached out her hand.

Happy watched as Prudence lifted her chin, so Nell could reach it better. The tabby studied Nell for some time. Then,

slowly, she closed her eyes and
leaned into her fingers.
Prudence showed Nell
just where to
scratch.

"Nell, honey!"
a voice called from
the other end of the barn. It was her father.
"It's time to head home."

"I have to go now," Nell whispered. "Thank
you for letting me pet you, Prudence." Then
she stood up and rushed down the aisle.
"Good-bye," she called.

Prudence leaped up and shook herself.
She looked over her shoulder toward
Happy's stall. When her glance met his, she
quickly turned around. She flicked her ears,
lifted her tail, and padded away.

Chapter Nine

The Best Hideout

"What do you mean, second thoughts?" Roscoe asked, tapping his foot on the floor of Happy's stall. "Now you *want* someone to buy you, so you have to leave Big Apple Barn?"

"That's not what I said at all," Happy argued. "I want to stay, but I'm not sure I want to run away."

"You're talking in circles," said Roscoe.

That's just what Happy had been thinking.

Maybe the plan didn't make any sense. Why run away from Big Apple Barn if he really wanted to stay? He wished he could have talked to Big Ben or Goldi, but he had not seen them in days.

"Well, fine. But you should know there's nothing I can do to stop those people if they come and you are in your stall. They'll take you away," Roscoe declared.

It was just before sunrise on Christmas Eve. In a couple of hours, Diane and her family would arrive to set up for the party. The guests would be there soon after. Happy and Roscoe were waiting for Prudence, so they could follow through with the plan. They wanted to do it before anyone at Diane's house woke up.

But there were still parts of the plan that made Happy nervous. For one thing, they would have to go outside to get to Roscoe's nest in the hay barn. What if someone saw them? And Happy wondered how big Roscoe's nest was. Was there enough room for Happy to hide?

"Did you explain the plan to Sassy?" Happy asked.

Roscoe nodded.

"Well, what did she say?" Happy was looking for a sign. He wanted to know he was doing the right thing.

Roscoe rolled his eyes. "She said it doesn't matter if you're hiding in the woods or the hay barn, you are still running away."

Happy sighed. Maybe Sassy was right.

"Come on," Roscoe said. "Let's stick to the plan."

"Let's see what Prudence says," suggested Happy.

Roscoe held the back of his paw to his forehead and sighed. "Oh, Happy. You're giving me a headache."

"That's funny," Prudence said as she approached Happy's stall. "Isn't it usually the other way around?"

"At last!" Roscoe said, scampering under the door. "Prudence, can you talk some sense into this pony? After all our hard work, Happy isn't sure he should run away."

Prudence gave Happy a curious look.

"You have to do it," Roscoe went on. "Remember what Prudence said? She doesn't want you to end up with a family that doesn't love you. Like what happened to her. You have to do it for Prudence."

Happy turned to Prudence. He wanted to hear it straight from her. He thought she might have changed her mind about Nell and her dad. Prudence took a breath, as if she was getting ready to say something, but then she stopped to listen. There was a ringing in the distance. It was a Christmas carol, coming from outside.

"Oh, no! We have to hurry!" Roscoe cried. "Diane's already awake! She always blasts music from her house before she sets up for the party. Prudence, get over here."

Prudence looked at Happy, then walked over to the door. Roscoe climbed onto her head. From there, he could just reach the lock on Happy's stall. Roscoe jammed his shoulder against the handle. "One, two, three," he grunted. The bolt slid to the side. As soon as Roscoe and Prudence were out of the way, Happy nudged the door open with his nose. He stepped out of his stall, then hesitated.

"Quick! To the hay barn!" Roscoe yelled. "We'll lose our chance!"

71

There wasn't enough time. *It's now or never,* Happy thought.

The mouse grabbed Happy's tail, and the pony bolted off at a canter.

Happy's charge down the barn aisle woke up many of the horses and ponies. Just over the clippity-clop of his hooves, he could hear his friends react. He was certain Sassy grumbled as he passed her stall, and Goldi called out in alarm, "Happy, come back!"

Happy tried to ignore them. Then he passed Big Ben's stall. The older horse did not say anything, but Happy saw something in his eyes. Happy wasn't sure what it was, so he kept running.

"You all right?" Happy asked, looking back at Roscoe. Roscoe held on tight as they rounded the corner, Happy's tail whizzing behind him.

The pair skidded to a stop in front of the large sliding barn door. Happy paused to catch his breath, then pushed at the door with his nose. Roscoe climbed Happy's tail and crawled up the pony's back until he was seated between Happy's ears. "Okay, once you get it open, run like crazy," the mouse directed.

The door felt cold against Happy's nose. It was heavier than he had expected. When it finally rolled to the side, a gust of wind whirled into the barn. Happy poked his head outside. He thought he would know that running away was the right thing to do as soon as he saw the hay barn. But he hardly noticed the hay barn, because he saw something else.

Snow. Everything was covered with snow! The hay barn, Diane's house, the apple tree, the picket fence. It was so fresh, the snow must have just fallen.

"Oh!" Happy exclaimed. "Look at the snow."

"Oh, no!" Roscoe exclaimed. "Look at the house!"

Happy tore his gaze from the wintry scene and focused on Diane's farmhouse.

"It's Diane!" Roscoe cried. "Look through that window. She's putting on her coat!"

A golden light shone through one of the house's windows. Happy could see his trainer pulling on a hat. Diane was headed for the barn! If Happy truly wanted to run away, he had to do it now.

"Quick, maybe she won't see us," Roscoe whispered in Happy's ear. "Run to the hay barn."

But Happy just stood in the doorway and looked out at the snow. He took a deep breath.

"Happy, you have to do something!" Roscoe insisted.

Just then, something small and sparkly

landed on Happy's nose and he knew exactly what to do. He closed his eyes tight and made a wish. When he opened his eyes again, the sky was filled with snowflakes — and Diane was opening the back door of the farmhouse. *There's still time*, Happy thought. He took one last look and spun around.

"Where are you going?" Roscoe asked, grabbing hold of Happy's ear to keep from tumbling off his head. "Do you know a better hiding place?"

"I do know a better place," Happy assured his friend as he cantered back into the barn. "It's the best."

Chapter Ten

Home for the Holidays

As Happy ran back into the barn, he looked into the stalls of each of his closest friends. Would he ever see them again? Big Ben and Goldi watched him go by with curiosity and concern. Sassy rolled her eyes. Then Happy trotted the rest of the way up the barn aisle and into his own stall. Roscoe didn't know what to say — for at least a second or two.

"*This* is the best hideout?" the mouse asked.

"I didn't say it was the best hideout," Happy reminded his friend. "I said it was the best place. And it is — the best place for me."

"Well, it's been nice knowing you, kid. I guess I'll be looking for a new best friend," Roscoe said, shaking his head sadly.

"Have a little faith, Roscoe," Happy said. "I have a feeling."

Roscoe began to walk around the edge of Happy's stall. "I do, too," he said. "It's hunger. So I'll at least stick around until you get fed. But I am not going to stay and watch you leave. I just can't."

"I'll stay," a voice promised. Happy had gotten used to Prudence chiming in on their conversations. He glanced around and saw her sitting on top of the stall door across

78

from his. "I knew you'd come back," she said.

Happy wanted to ask what she meant, but just then Diane came rushing into the barn. She was murmuring to herself. "The door was wide open. Are all the horses here? Did they get too cold?" She looked into every stall and then stopped in front of Happy's door. She gave him a long look. "Happy, your door is unlatched," she announced. "It's a good thing you didn't get loose. We have big plans for you today." Diane bolted Happy's door and went on to check the other stalls.

Big plans? Happy wasn't sure he liked the sound of that. Were the big plans that she was selling him?

"That's it," Roscoe said glumly. "Now you're stuck. Prudence and I can't get you out again, not with people around."

"It's okay." Happy knew that coming back

to his stall was the right thing to do. Now, he would just have to wait for Nell and her father to arrive. Then he would know if he got to stay at Big Apple Barn and be a lesson pony, or if he would have a new home.

Roscoe stayed until after Diane came by with Happy's grain. He nibbled at a piece of corn. "I guess I'm not hungry after all," he said. "See you later, I hope." Roscoe gave Happy a half-smile and walked away.

Before long, the party had started. The air was filled with the smell of apple cider and the sound of holiday music. Diane, Ivy, and the rest of their family rushed around to make sure everything was in place and everyone was having fun. Happy's students visited him one by one, each with a treat and a loving pat. Happy enjoyed seeing everyone in such a festive mood, but he did not feel like he could celebrate. He kept waiting for Nell and her dad to arrive.

Happy stamped his foot and swayed his head from side to side. It was what he did when he was nervous.

"They'll be here," Prudence said, watching Happy closely. It was already afternoon. Happy didn't think he could wait much longer.

Then Happy saw Nell round the corner. She looked like she might burst with excitement. She rushed to his stall.

"You'll never guess what!" Nell said to Happy, trying to stay quiet so she didn't scare the other horses. "My dad gave me my big present today, and it is right here. In this very barn."

Happy swallowed hard. This was it.

"Oh, Prudence," Nell said to the cat, who had jumped up on Happy's stall door. "I'm glad you're here. I can tell you both." Nell took a deep breath. "I can *show* you both."

Happy and Prudence looked at each other.

"I got a kitten!" Nell said, unzipping her coat with one hand. In the other, she cradled a tiny orange kitten to her chest. "That's why I was late. We were picking her out. Diane's the one who told my dad about the litter. It was at another barn."

A kitten? Happy thought. *A kitten!*

"I know it is a lot of work to raise a kitten." Nell smiled at Prudence, who was giving Nell and the kitten a long, hard look. "But I can do it." When Nell turned to Happy, he was still shocked. "Happy, don't worry. I still like ponies. But a kitten can sleep on my bed. A pony can't do that."

As Nell held her kitten with one hand, she reached out to pet Prudence with the other. Her father walked up and put his hand on her shoulder. "So this is the cat you like so much," he said. "I hope this kitten will make you just as happy."

"I have a feeling she will," said Nell, smiling at her dad. "And maybe she will grow up to be like Prudence. I think Prudence is wise. She seems picky about her friends, but loyal. And that's a good way to be." She petted the scruffy tabby a while longer.

"Yes, that's very *prudent* of her," Nell's dad said with a chuckle. "Now we should get you and your new kitten home."

Nell tickled Prudence's chin one more time, then pulled a carrot out of her pocket for Happy. After he ate his treat, she rubbed Happy's nose to say good-bye. She reached out and grabbed her father's arm. Happy and Prudence watched her leave.

"You knew, didn't you?" Happy asked.

"Let's just say I had a feeling, too," the cat said. "After getting to know them, I knew Nell and her dad were good people. They wouldn't do anything rash. They both know a pet isn't a present, it's a friend." Prudence sat up straight and raised her chin. "I think that kitten will be as happy with Nell as I am here."

"I hope so," Happy said. Now that he knew Nell and her dad weren't buying him, he should have felt relieved. But Diane said she had big plans for Happy today. What could they be? Happy had a hard time enjoying the rest of the party. Prudence had left and he felt suddenly alone.

"Why so serious, Happy?" Ivy asked as she walked up to the pony's stall. She was holding a big, white box tied with a silver ribbon. "I have a present for you," she said. "It might cheer you up."

Happy put his head over the door and whinnied. He was glad to see Ivy. She made him feel like everything would be all right.

"Take a look," said Ivy. She lifted the lid and pulled out a bright red horse blanket. "Come on, let me put it on you."

Ivy led Happy out of his stall. He stood quietly as she put the blanket on his back and buckled all of the straps.

"He looks marvelous," Diane said. As she spoke, she stared Happy in the eye. "You know, a funny thing happened this morning," she told Ivy. "I thought I saw a pony standing by the front door of the barn. It looked a lot like Happy. And when

I checked the stalls, his was unlocked. I must have been imagining things." Diane shrugged. "You don't think he'd get loose, and then come back to his stall, do you?"

Ivy looked at her mother with wide eyes. She shrugged right back.

"I'm glad he's still here," the trainer said, giving Happy a knowing look. "Our plan wouldn't work very well without him, would it?" Diane scratched Happy behind the ears. "Now get him ready. I'll see you outside."

"We have to hurry," Ivy said, turning to Happy. "Everyone's waiting for you."

Happy was so confused. Why was he going outside? Was he being sold after all? His mind spun as Ivy combed his mane and hooked a lead to his halter. "You look wonderful," she said as she led him down the aisle to the big barn door.

When she rolled the door open, Happy looked outside. There was Diane with tall Big Ben, Andrea with Sassy, Ivy and Andrea's dad with Goldi, and Prudence. Plus, there was a man in a heavy coat and rubber boots holding a camera.

"We're taking a holiday photo, Happy," Ivy said. "In the snow! Come on."

Just before Happy stepped outside, he felt a gentle tug on his tail. He looked back and saw Roscoe climbing up onto his back, just as he had done that morning.

"Let's go, Happy," encouraged Ivy. Happy lifted his hoof high and watched it sink into the deep blanket of snow. Brrr!

By now, Roscoe had made his way to his favorite perch right between Happy's ears. "So I hear you're staying!" Roscoe whispered. "That's the best news. I knew everything would be fine," he said. "You really worry too much."

Happy shook his head — very lightly, of course, because he didn't want Roscoe to fall off. As Ivy walked him up to the group, he lowered his head. He suddenly felt embarrassed. What would his friends say about his attempt to run away?

"Oh, Happy," Goldi began, "Sassy told us everything. We're so glad you were not sold."

"Yes, and we're glad you didn't run away," Big Ben added. "It wouldn't be right, leaving without saying good-bye."

"Of course he didn't run away," Sassy insisted, her mane blowing in the wind. "Because he knew I was right. Running away doesn't solve anything."

Happy tried to look shocked. "Why

would anyone ever run away from Big Apple Barn?" he asked.

"Exactly," Sassy replied with a smirk.

As the friends laughed, Happy realized the other horses had on red blankets, too.

"The horses are all wearing Big Apple Barn red," Andrea said.

Diane smiled. "Of course. They're all part of our family!"

All of a sudden, Happy got chills. And not from the snow, but from what Diane had said. He really *was* part of the Big Apple Barn family!

The people and horses moved around so the man with the camera could see everyone. Happy pricked his ears forward as he looked at his horse friends, Ivy and her family, Prudence, and Roscoe. And when the cameraman asked them to say "candy canes," Happy knew that life at Big Apple Barn could not be sweeter. It was going to be a happy holiday after all.

Horse Sense

How can you tell what a horse or pony is thinking? They often give us clues through their body language.

When a horse **pins his ears back** and **flashes the whites of his eyes,** it is an unhappy response. The horse might feel sick or threatened. It's a warning — be careful.

When a pony has her **ears pricked forward,** she is interested. Usually, it is a sign that the pony is in a good mood. It can also show curiosity or fear.

If a pony has **one ear cocked,** he is listening. This often happens when a horse is being ridden, and it shows that he is paying attention to his rider.

Pawing at the ground is a way a horse says she's impatient. At feeding time, a barn is full of pawing horses, anxious for their food!

A **swish of the tail** means something is not quite right. The pony might be annoyed, by a fly or by another horse.

When a horse is excited, he seems to **stand taller.** He raises his tail, lifts his head, and looks wide awake.

You can learn more by simply studying a pony's expressions. Horses have emotions and moods, just like people. You should always be sensitive to how a horse is feeling. It's the best way to build a true friendship!